BRUCE HALE

Big Bad Baby

illustrated by
STEVE BREEN

DIAL BOOKS FOR YOUNG READERS
an imprint of Penguin Group (USA) LLC

For Adela, Kim, and Hoku—
the wild bunch
—B.H.

For Daniel
—S.B.

DIAL BOOKS FOR YOUNG READERS
Published by the Penguin Group • Penguin Group (USA) LLC, 375 Hudson Street, New York, NY 10014

USA | Canada | UK | Ireland | Australia | New Zealand | India | South Africa | China | penguin.com

A PENGUIN RANDOM HOUSE COMPANY

Text copyright © 2014 by Bruce Hale • Illustrations copyright © 2014 by Steve Breen

Library of Congress Cataloging-in-Publication Data • Hale, Bruce. • Big Bad Baby/Bruce Hale ; illustrated by Steve Breen.
pages cm • Summary: When Sweet Little Sammy suddenly turns into Big Bad Baby, nothing can stop his misbehavior—or that of his evil hench-dog, Boris—except, perhaps, his mother, armed with his favorite blue blanky.
ISBN 978-0-8037-3585-9 (hardcover) • [1. Behavior-Fiction. 2. Babies-Fiction. 3. Blankets-Fiction.] I. Breen, Steve, illustrator.
II. Title. PZ7.H1295Bhm 2014 [E]-dc23 2013027092

Manufactured in China on acid-free paper • 10 9 8 7 6 5 4 3 2 1
Designed by Jason Henry • Text set in Grumble • The artwork for this book was created with india ink, water colors, and colored pencil.
The publisher does not have any control over and does not assume any responsibility for author or third-party websites or their content.

No one knows how, no one knows why. Maybe Sweet Little Sammy's applesauce was just a wee bit too tart. Maybe his nap was delayed just a wee bit too long. Maybe his favorite blue blanky was in the wash.

But whatever the reason, one warm spring day, Sweet Little Sammy turned into . . .

Bad Baby!

He chased the cat . . .

And he redecorated
the kitchen . . .

But that wasn't *nearly*
enough trouble for Bad Baby.

He needed bigger and better badness.

"Ba-ba doo *dee* boo," Bad Baby told his evil hench-dog, Boris. (Which in bad baby talk means, "We'll show them! We'll show them all!")

"Woof," said Boris.

Off they crawled to cook up some serious badness.
And after a few false starts, Bad Baby hatched the perfect plan.
He laughed a bad, bad baby laugh—

"mwah-ha-hee-hee-hee!"

—built the perfect Monster Machine, and pushed the button.

And with a *wooka wooka wooka* and a *chooka chooka choo* . . .
Out popped . . .

Pausing only to slurp from his sippy cup, Big Bad Baby set out to take over the world!

He made a ruckus
in the neighborhood.

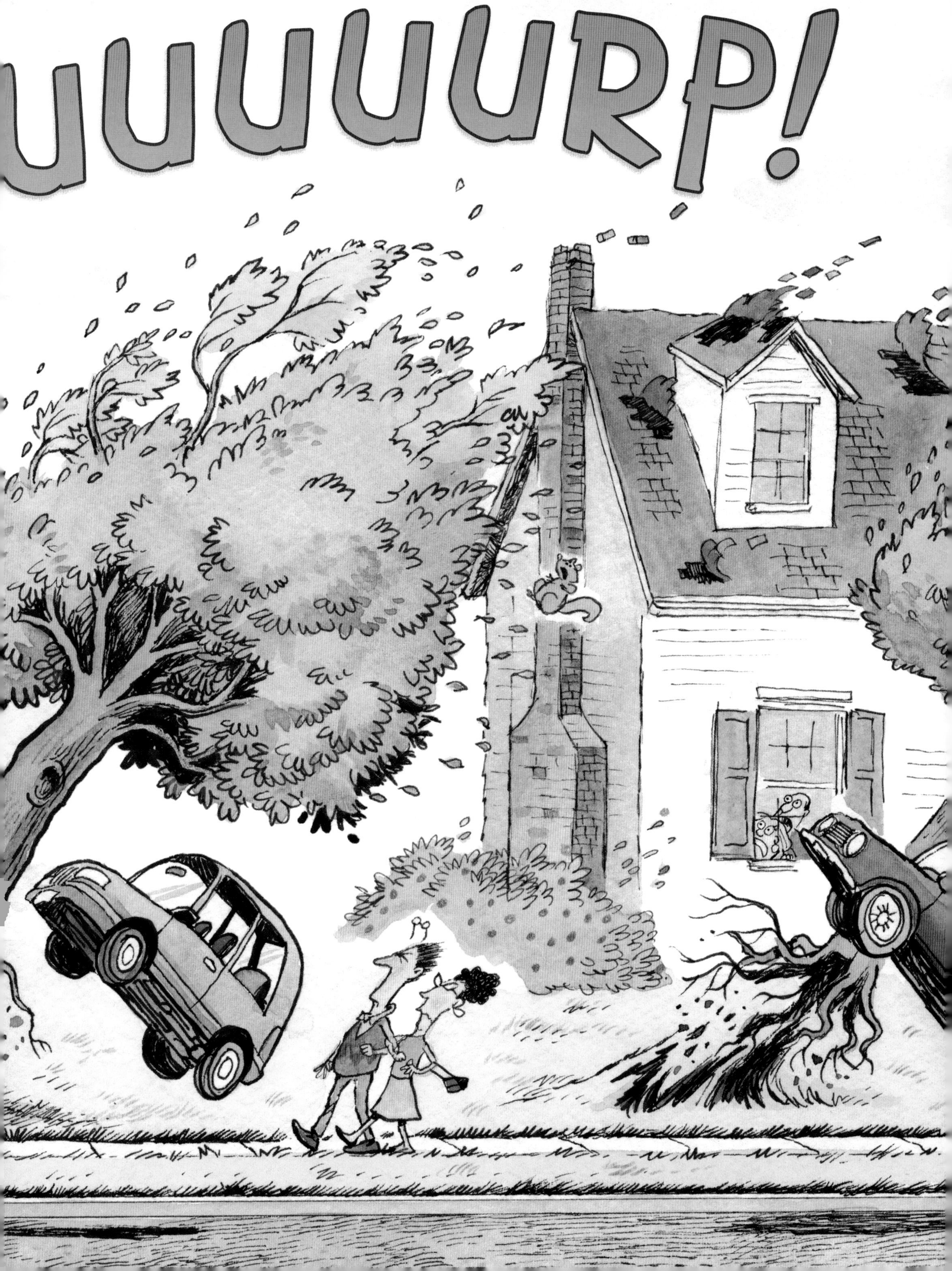
UUUUURP!

He played rough with toys.

He colored outside the lines.

And he made a real mess.

Not the fire department.

Not even the librarians and
their sweet stories could stop him.

But then . . .
With a *wooka wooka wooka* and a *chooka chooka choo* . . . Mom sprung a surprise.

"*Aah! Wah-wah boo!*" cried Big Bad Baby.
(Which in bad baby talk means, "No! Not the blanky!")
Down dropped the Mega-Blanky with a *WHUMP!*
"WAH!" cried Big Bad Baby.
"Woof," said Boris.

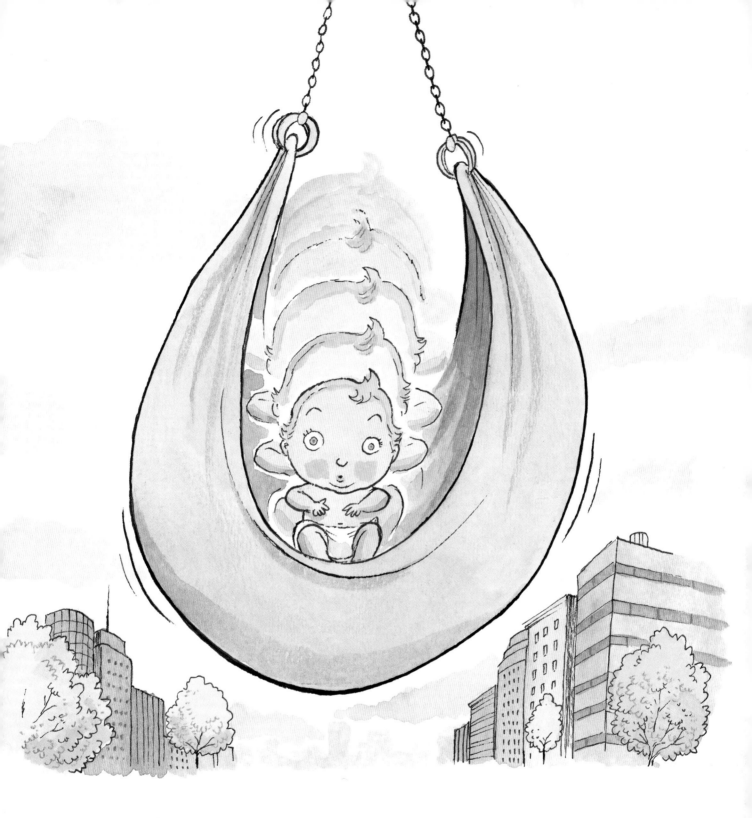

Those choppers whirred and they chirred, and they
wrapped up Big Bad Baby, snug as a big bad bug in a rug.

Then the lead chopper picked up Big Bad Baby and flew
him back through town, back down his path of destruction,
back to his home . . .

. . . for a warm bottle of milk and a snuggle.

"Big bad babies need love too," said Sammy's mom, wrapping him in his favorite blue blanky.

"Gee-gah goo," sighed Sweet Little Sammy.
Which in bad, bad baby talk means . . .